Hedgehog Queen

Hedgehog Queen

David Hills

The Book Guild Ltd

First published in Great Britain in 2018 by
The Book Guild Ltd
9 Priory Business Park
Wistow Road, Kibworth
Leicestershire, LE8 0RX
Freephone: 0800 999 2982
www.bookguild.co.uk
Email: info@bookguild.co.uk
Twitter: @bookguild

Typeset in Minion Pro

Printed and bound in Great Britain by CPI Group (UK) Ltd, Croydon, CR0 4YY

ISBN 978 1912362 455

British Library Cataloguing in Publication Data.
A catalogue record for this book is available from the British Library.

For,
Jill.
My mum and dad.
Louisa (Jill's mum).
Auntie Delia and Uncle Bill.

And a special thank you to the hedgehogs in my garden for giving me the magic for this story…

The Awakening

Light rain fell gently on to the scattered woodpile.

Inside, little eyes opened and a nose began to twitch. A hedgehog woke from his winter sleep.

Suddenly he sneezed and covered the inside of his winter home with a glittering, sparkling dust.

He moved into position to leave this safe and dry

hideaway in search of food, friendship, happiness, and above all the search for 'the chosen one'.

After emerging into the darkening damp evening, he could feel the light rain on his nose.

He looked up to the sky, smiled, shook his head and continued, leaving a tiny little trail of sparkle dust behind him.

Creeping quietly through the undergrowth he found himself coming upon a cold hard surface. "What is this?" he asked himself. It was a grey path but looked black in the fading light.

"I think it is going to be a magical evening," he whispered.

He looked around, sticking his wiggly nose up in to the air to detect… well, anything.

On continuing across the black ground, he found himself faced with a large wooden rectangle in front of him.

The hedgehog inspected this strange object. There was a small gap between the wood and the wet ground. A very slight change in light appeared under the wood.

I can get under there, thought the hedgehog. He lowered his body and gently caught the top of spikes on the base of what was a gate; this tickled the hedgehog and he looked back over his shoulder, giggling.

Then he stopped, listened, and sniffed at the air. Throwing his sparkle all around the garden, he sniffed all the ground and he came across a small woody pathway. This was perfect for the hedgehog to follow.

He skipped and ran fast down the path until he came across a large log. He stopped, peeped over it... and with one big bounce, and a little sparkle dust, he was over and on his way.

He hurried through the garden, looking for adventure.

Everywhere he went he continued to leave this sparkling
magical dust trail.

Alistair

A little boy opened his eyes. The room was quiet and dark. "Must still be night time," he whispered.

He sat up in his bed and stared out of the window.

It was dark, but something inside him told him to go to the window and look out.

Yes, still very dark, he thought. He looked down at the low lights in the garden.

Alistair was a shy and quiet little boy, however, he always thought that he had a special power. He was able to relate to animals and understand what they need; this was generally kindness, and sometimes help. He thinks of them all as his wonderful, magical friends.

Unfortunately, he had recently said goodbye to Toby, the fat, furry black cat that he had said, so often, was his best friend. Toby had passed away due to old age.

Due to this, he found himself a weeny bit lonely.

He continued to stare out of the window. He was

about to turn and return to his bed when, suddenly, he saw the glittering, sparkling trail all around the garden. Then he spotted a small moving shape.

"It is a hedgehog," Alistair commented gently, "but what is all this shiny dust? It must have come in from under the gate, as it looks as if the sparkling dust begins there."

WOW, this is great, he thought.

Immediately the little boy ran out of his room, down the stairs and out into the garden.

"HELLO!" he shouted.

A Magical Evening

The little boy looked down and saw the light scatter of glitter dust left by this fascinating creature.

He was in wonder of this amazing, sparkling, fast-moving little bubbly hedgehog. *Where is it now?* he thought.

The next thing he knew, the hedgehog appeared. The little boy watched intensely as the hedgehog ran around searching. *Searching for what?*

Laughing and smiling from ear to ear, his spikes were long and constantly moving in a forward and backwards motion, and the tip of every spike was sparkling and shiny.

The little boy moved toward the hedgehog; he was also excited and gave a big yell.

"WOW, WOW, WOWWWWWW," he screamed.

The boy sat down on the little garden seat and puffed; he was a little out of breath with excitement.

The hedgehog continued racing around the garden.

Then... the hedgehog spotted the little boy.

A little bit cautious, the hedgehog crept toward him.

"Hello," said the hedgehog with his deep, warm voice. The little boy stared in disbelief at what he was seeing and hearing.

"You can talk?" asked the little boy.

"Yes, of course I can talk," replied the hedgehog, and he laughed, happily.

"Who are you, little man?" said the hedgehog.

"My... name... is... Alistair," the little boy replied slowly

"Then you can be my new friend," said the hedgehog. "You run and I will chase you?"

"WAIT!" Alistair replied. "Who are you?"

"I am Hamish and I am the MAGIC HEDGEHOG and you are my new friend, are you happy...?" Hamish asked.

"Yes, yes, oh yes," replied Alistair in a hurry. "I really want to be your friend."

"Excellent," said Hamish, "then run." With that, Alistair began running at speed toward the bottom of the garden.

He looked behind himself. "Can't catch me!" he shouted back at the hedgehog, who was fast approaching.

"Yes, I can," screamed Hamish. "Yes, I can."

Then, a large puff of silver sparkly dust filled the air and Alistair stopped.

"Got you!" screamed Hamish. "Got you!"

Hamish rolled over on to his back, laughing and puffing and smiling. "Got you," he said once again.

There was a brief silence. "OK, you got me, Hamish – or should I call you Mr Sparkle?" Alistair asked jokingly.

"Now I will get you." With that, Alistair quickly turned and ran straight at the hedgehog. Hamish bounced up in to the air and, within seconds, had disappeared.

Alistair stared around the garden for a second and then shouted, "Hey, hey, that is cheating."

"No… it is not," replied Hamish. Alistair could hear him but could not see him.

Then he heard Hamish laugh softly. Alistair crept toward the corner of the garden where he knew Hamish was hiding.

"BOO!" shouted Hamish, and he gave another big puff of sparkle.

At speed Hamish was away and zipping around the garden, "You will never catch me!" screamed Hamish, excitedly.

Alistair went back to the little chair to sit and watch this wonderful creature, run, bounce, skip and eventually disappear.

All went quiet and Alistair yawned and then called out, "Good night, Mr Sparkle. I've got to go back to bed. I'll see you again very soon?" Alistair asked hopefully and happily.

"Yes," replied Hamish, wherever he was.

"This was great fun," Alistair called out as he left the garden.

The Next Evening

Hamish had once again arrived in Alistair's garden, knowing he could have fun and adventure here.

Hamish called out for Alistair and waited patiently for him to appear.

At that moment Hamish saw something creeping toward him, but it was not Alistair. He felt light warm air on his long nose and could hear a small sniffing sound.

The shape then moved a short distance away from the hedgehog. Hamish was not sure what to do at this moment. So, he waited, and then he saw it was a little black cat.

"Hello, little black cat…" whispered Hamish.

The little cat stared at Hamish, gave a small meow and then ran away.

At that moment Alistair came running up the path. "Hello, Hamish, hello."

Hamish was pleased to see him so he bounced into the air and a little puff of sparkle appeared.

"What are you doing?" asked Alistair.

Hamish told him all about the little black cat.

"Oh yes, he lives next door," said Alistair.

"Next door?" Hamish asked, not understanding.

"That house," Alistair pointed to another house, "over there," he said.

"I see," said Hamish.

"Goodbye, Alistair," Hamish said, unexpectedly.

"What? Where are you going and why?" Alistair questioned, a little confused. "You just called me out to play…"

"Well, I will be back, but I need something to eat and then we can play… yes?"

"Wait!" said Alistair, and with that he ran down the path in to his house.

He soon returned with a small bag of peanuts. "Here, little man," he said, "try these."

Hamish crunched one at speed. "Mmmm, very good. More, please?" Alistair chuckled, pleased that Hamish was happy, he then gave him a small handful of them.

Alistair smiled with pleasure as the hedgehog crunched through the peanuts. He could see that Hamish liked them.

"This is great," commented Alistair. "I now have a new friend."

They were both very happy.

Hamish quickly finished his meal, and then asked, "Water?"

"In the pond, silly," replied Alistair.

"Oh yes, of course," said Hamish, feeling rather silly. They both laughed together.

Hamish made a quick dash toward the pond. He turned the corner and descended gently. "WATER, YES… I found it."

He moved into position, stretched his head in a forward and down movement, and then, splash! He's nose was in the water. He began to drink. Sparkly ripples moved out across the water's surface as the hedgehog took each mouthful of water. He stayed in this position for the next few minutes, enjoying the fresh cold liquid.

"Wow! Look at the water," cried Alistair, "it is all shiny."

"Are you happy now?" asked Alistair.

"Yes, this is a magical garden," said Hamish.

"I knew it, I knew it," continued Hamish. "All I need is here, including you…" Hamish, was smiling.

With this, Alistair bent down and gently stroked the little hedgehog. Hamish giggled as this tickled him.

"Oooohhhh, you are prickly."

Then Alistair stroked him again and again and soon the hedgehog was giggling loud. "Stop it, stop it," he said. "It tickles."

After a long time of tickling and running around the garden, Alistair heard his mum calling him to go into the house.

"I got to go, and you can come too, yes?"

"Not today but yes, soon I hope… I too need to sleep," replied Hamish.

With that Alistair bent down and gently patted Hamish. "Good night, Mr Sparkle," he joked. Hamish bounced, left a flash of sparkle, and disappeared.

Alistair went in his house to bed.

A couple of minutes passed and Hamish found himself in the dark corner of the garden; he curled into a ball of inch-long sparkling spikes and fell asleep.

Alistair's Care

After getting ready for bed, cleaning his teeth and putting on his pyjamas, Alistair jumped in to his bed. His mum went to close the curtains. "Can you leave them open? Please, Mum!" Alistair said.

"Yes, if you want that... OK. Why?" she asked. Alistair did not tell her, but it was because of Hamish he wanted the curtains open. It made him feel like he was still with him.

Alistair lay in his soft warm bed and started to remember all that had happened over the last two days.

Then a thought came to him: *I wonder where he goes when he is not in my garden? I wonder why he has all that sparkle dust.* Going back to the first thought: *If I get a box for him, he can stay in the garden. That will be nice.*

"That is, it. Decision made: I will get him a box."

The next morning came and Alistair awoke and sat up in his bed quickly. "I need a box," he whispered.

With that he jumped out of bed, washed himself and got dressed all within five minutes. He went down stairs and started his search for the box.

He looked all around the house in all of the rooms, but nothing was good enough. He went to the garage and then suddenly, under an old blanket, was a small wooden box with a square hole at the bottom.

"Perfect," he shouted.

He grabbed it and rushed to the corner of the garden where Hamish had been hiding earlier. He looked about and called, "Hamish? Are you here?"

Alistair could not see or hear him, but this did not stop him; he took great care placing the box in the sheltered quiet area of the garden.

"There!" he said to himself.

"Looks perfect. Hamish will be pleased."

The little boy then shouted out, "This is for you, Hamish, wherever you are. I will see you later."

A New Home

In the scattered woodpile, Hamish awoke and laid there for a few seconds, remembering his adventures over the last two days.

Could Alistair be the Chosen One? wondered, the hedgehog. *If he continues to be the kind and caring boy he seems to be, then yes*, noted Hamish to himself.

"I must go and find him," he said.

Soon he was in Alistair's garden, but what was that in the corner? "That is new. What is it?"

Hamish hurried toward the box at speed. He stopped at the little square opening and then puffed some sparkling dust inside.

"Looks good," he chuckled, and continued into the wooden box. "Wow, this is fantastic. Yes, this will be perfect; I will live here, I think," said Hamish. "Live in Alistair's garden, yes. Whoopee."

Suddenly he heard, "You like it then I see?" grinned Alistair.

"Yes, it is perfect."

"Yes, I thought so," said Alistair excitedly. "I got it for you."

"Thank you, Alistair, thank you. You, are a thoughtful little boy."

Then a noise came from behind them. They both turned and looked down the garden.

From nowhere another hedgehog came in to the garden and it was speeding around the pond, not stopping for anything. It moved at speed in a large circle around the pond and disappeared quickly back under the gate and out of the garden.

"Who is that?" Alistair asked.

"Not sure," replied Hamish.

"Why was there no sparkling dust and shiny spikes like you have got?" asked Alistair.

"Well, I told you: I am... the... MAGIC HEDGEHOG."

One Evening

Hamish ventured out of his new home.

He made his way around the pond and then quickly came to a halt as the little black cat was in his way.

The cat was staring hard at a flower by the pond; he was watching a frog moving in it. The cat turned to the hedgehog, stared at him and sniffed him, but did not move. The cat looked back towards the flower.

Hamish decided he would go on to the lawn and go around the cat.

Three steps and Hamish was on the lawn.

He moved in a circular motion round the little black cat. Then, Hamish stepped on to another frog that was lying in the grass.

The frog leapt up into the air over the cat; the cat saw it, and then leaped up in the air after the frog.

The frog landed in the pond and the cat landed on the flower and nearly fell in to the pond itself. Hamish was amazed; he bounced and puffed some of his magical sparkle over them all. He chuckled and giggled.

Hamish continued his evening stroll down the garden and thought, *I will have a quick drink of water before Alistair arrives, as I am sure he will be chasing me and we will be running and jumping later so I will get thirsty.*

The hedgehog lapped eagerly at the water, which struck him to be almost warm water tonight.

Without warning Hamish felt something knock into him with force. The next thing he knew he was in the water.

Hamish paddled quickly in the deep water and kept his head and nose pointing up in the air. He puffed some of his sparkling dust up in to the air and the shiny water got warmer.

Then, he was surprised to see that there was another hedgehog in the water with him, struggling to keep a float and in the same situation as him.

At that moment, Hamish found himself being lifted gently. Then he began to scratch and grab at the grey stone rocks surrounding the pond.

Eventually he got a grip on the stone and made his way to the dry ground. That gentle lift helped him. He bounced up into the air to dry himself off.

What had happened?

Why was there another hedgehog in the water?

Where is that other hedgehog?

All these questions dashed through the hedgehog's thoughts.

Hamish soon realised that another hedgehog had come at speed under the gate to get some water and had bashed into Hamish and knocked him in to the pond. The force was so great that both of them fell in to the water.

Then, the second hedgehog was also being lifted gently. Soon this one too was on the safe soil.

Hamish shook himself down and looked around for the other hedgehog, who was obviously a little bit crazy and playful; however, it was extremely quiet and Hamish found himself alone.

Hamish could not find it. "Must, have run away," he said to himself.

On the water's surface was a little sparkle dust, and something small and gold was sitting at the bottom of the pond.

Hamish recognised this at once and then, surprised, said, "I know what that is… Where is Alistair?" He was talking to himself.

At that moment Alistair appeared.

"I had to wash my hands," said Alistair.

"Well, you missed all that," said Hamish.

Hamish told Alistair all that had just happened and how pleased he was that the two hedgehogs got help.

Alistair giggled, "Really? Mr Sparkle, I wonder who helped you."

"I know," said Hamish, "the clue is in the bottom of the pond."

Alistair stopped giggling and a frown came across his face. "What do… you… mean?" asked Alistair.

"You will see," replied Hamish.

Alistair smiled and said, "That is good. Are you OK?"

"Yes, I am fine now, but my sparkle is a little damp.... I will dry out soon!"

The Next Evening

Alistair came home from school and rushed into the garden, looking for the wonderful Mr Sparkle, Hamish the magic hedgehog. The garden was very quiet and there was no sign of him.

Alistair made his way to the little house. The house was there but quiet.

"Hamish," Alistair called, "are you in there?"

No sound, no movement, and no sparkle. Alistair became a little sad. "Where has he gone?" whispered Alistair, disappointed.

Searching...

The next day the little boy returned once again to the garden. It seemed colder that evening.

The little boy wandered slowly around the garden, up to the pond, up to where the hedgehog home was positioned.

He turned and was about to leave and give up his hunt when suddenly...

"Hello..." said a deep warm voice, Alistair recognised it instantly.

"Hamish? Hamish? Is that you?" The little boy turned his head at speed and looked behind him. "Is that you Hamish?" Alistair asked again.

He saw nothing.

Then, again, "Hello?"

At that moment, deep in the dark sheltered area of the hedgehog's home was movement.

The little boy strained his eyes in the darkness to

see what it was. Then, suddenly, it appeared that the hedgehog's house was growing.

"Growing?" said Alistair to himself. "WOW!" he muttered.

The boy stared in wonder and amazement as the hedgehog's house got bigger, bigger and then even bigger.

Soon it was as big as the house the boy lived in.

Amazed, Alistair stared. At that moment, the box lit up and the boy could see the entrance. It was now twice the size of him.

"Hello!" he heard once again. He knew now it was coming from inside the hedgehog's home.

"Come in," the deep warm voice said, "come in, come in."

The little boy ran to the entrance…

The little boy stopped at the entrance…

The light was bright and he could hear distant music. This appeared to be coming from within the hedgehog's home.

"Come on, come in…" said the voice again, encouragingly.

"Hamish… is that you?" called Alistair.

Alistair made his way slowly, cautiously, and a little nervously, through the entrance and entered the home of this wonderful creature.

He walked through what appeared to be a passageway. He looked down and then noticed that the soiled wood base of the box had become a soft, deep-red carpet.

It is wonderful, Alistair smiled.

Eventually the passage turned to the left.

The little boy continued.

The music was getting louder, clearer.

He entered a room, a big room, and there in front of him he saw a very long table.

The table, made of solid wood, had a perfectly polished finish and shone in the light.

It was so shiny that Alistair could see himself in it.

It is warm and very cosy, thought the little boy.

"WOW!" he muttered.

"Hello!" said the little boy, and there he saw him, Hamish, Mr Sparkle himself, was there to meet him.

"HELLO, young man," said the hedgehog, who then gave a big puff of sparkle that covered Alistair. Hamish chuckled with mischievous fun and then smiled widely.

Alistair too giggled at this and then replied quickly.

"Hello, Hamish." The little boy had the tiniest tear in his eye, he was so pleased to see Hamish again.

"Follow me," said Hamish.

The little boy followed and asked, "Where are we going?"

"Not far… follow me," Hamish said.

They walked around, in what appeared to be a circle, and then the hedgehog said, "Look behind you."

Alistair turned and to his amazement the table was now highly decorated.

The crystal glasses and silver goblets, the shiny silver knives, forks and spoons shone and glinted in the light of the hundreds of candles that were burning brightly on the massive cake, which had been strategically placed in the dead centre of this huge and wonderful looking table.

The table was now covered in the little boy's favourite foods. There were hot thick chips, sausages, burgers, chicken nuggets, fish fingers.

There was also lots of ice cream, of all colours, flavours with crunchy wafer biscuits to go with them.

"Wow!" shouted Alistair.

There was cola, lemonade, orange juice and cream soda; these were some other very special favourites of the boy's.

"This is all for you…" said the hedgehog, who began to chuckle.

"Me?" said the boy. "Me? Really?"

The little boy was excited, and full of wonder.

"Why?" Alistair asked softly.

"Well, you have not noticed but the clock has just turned twelve midnight and it is now your birthday. This is your birthday party. This is for you, my very dear friend," said Hamish the hedgehog.

The little boy ran to the hedgehog and hugged him.

Suddenly the spikes on the hedgehog's body were soft and did not hurt the boy at all.

Then the boy rushed to the table and grabbed some of those golden brown, hot, chunky and tasty chips.

Alistair grinned with enormous happiness.

He began to eat, chip after chip.

The hedgehog smiled and said softly, "Slow down, little man, slow down… The chips will never end."

The little boy frowned and asked, "What does that mean?"

"It means," continued the hedgehog, "the food will never be finished; it will last as long as it is required."

"How is that possible?" Alistair asked.

"Am I not the MAGIC HEDGEHOG?" questioned Hamish, smiling.

"WAIT…!" said Hamish. The boy stopped eating, the music stopped and all went dark for a few seconds; then, without any warning, the room was filled with light, music and lots of other hedgehogs.

There must have been twenty or thirty in total, but it difficult to tell as they were running and jumping.

They were smiling, laughing and hugging each other.

They all stopped and stared at Alistair.

"HELLO," they all said loudly to the little boy.

Again, it went quiet.

The little boy looked at all the hedgehogs.

"Will you… join… us?" he said in his shy way.

With that all the hedgehogs cheered loudly, and all the hedgehogs battled their way to the table and pushed, barged, smiled and laughed their way to the banquet before them.

The music was loud and the noise of the hedgehogs enjoying themselves and eating was powerful.

They were laughing, smiling, eating, drinking and dancing.

The little boy looked on; he could not believe it. He then noted that previously he had assumed that all the hedgehogs looked the same. That was until now.

Now the boy could see they were all different: some had a longer nose, some had bigger eyes, some had glasses, some had grey spikes, some had black spikes, some were very big others not so big.

He then noticed that none of these hedgehogs had sparkle. He grinned widely and remembered what Hamish had continually said – "I am the MAGIC HEDGEHOG."

"My dear friends," the little boy shouted.

Then, silence.

The music stopped the talking stopped and the hedgehogs stopped.

The little boy looked on. Scared of what he had just said.

"Please stand," a voice said loudly and respectively.

All the hedgehogs where up from their chairs, the floor or anywhere else they had been enjoying themselves.

The light dulled and there was a feeling of wonder, expectation and nervousness around the table.

Then in came a large, slow-moving figure from the shadows with what appeared to be a golden crown on its head.

Large cheers came from the room.

It was a hedgehog, larger than anything else in the room.

This hedgehog glided in slowly.

The impressive crown was shining and twinkling in the now soft candlelight.

"The light is soft like the lights in the garden," the little boy remembered.

"Who is that?" whispered, Alistair to Hamish.

"That is the Hedgehog Queen," replied Hamish. "She has lived forever and there is nothing she does not know."

The little boy could feel the respect they all had for the QUEEN.

The queen hedgehog positioned herself at the end of the table; she sat on a large, red, silk-covered throne. She nodded her head and the party continued.

Music, food and drink were being shared.

Laughter, dancing and fun was had by all.

Then

Then the queen stood. Silence once again hit the room.

"The queen wishes to speak to the little boy," said the rather small hedgehog to the right of the queen.

The little boy become a tiny bit nervous.

"Please come forward," the queen hedgehog said gently.

The boy made his way to the queen.

Something inside him made him bow.

"ALISTAIR! Be proud, you have proven yourself to be kind, considerate and, above all, honest.

"You have protected us all in your garden, you have provided us with food, and you have given us a wonderful place to live that is dry safe and comfortable. In addition to this, you, saved me and your loyal friend from the pool of water in your garden. Of course, we would have got out," she said jokingly

"You lifted us gently to dry land…"

The boy remembered back, and yes, yes. "Wow! That was you?" the boy asked slowly with surprise in his voice.

The situation the little boy now found himself in was strange, exciting and amazing.

"Yes," replied the queen, smiling. "I too go outside to explore and have fun." She grinned.

The queen stood proud and happy. "To say a big thank you to you for the consideration, effort and your caring for us as you do. I now wish to pass to you this special, special thank you."

Alistair did not know what to say or do. He looked down but was unable to make out, at first, what the queen was holding.

He looked hard at it, it looked like some sort of gold, metal object.

"Please come this way," said the queen.

As the boy moved closer, the queen moved elegantly to the little boy.

They met.

Alistair naturally knelt in front of the hedgehog queen.

"Let it be known that today, on his birthday, all the hedgehogs in the world wish to thank Allister for his actions of kindness to us. I therefore present you with this lovely gold badge that makes you Protector of Hedgehogs always."

The badge was bright, shiny gold. It had the image of the hedgehog queen wearing her crown on the font and 'Alistair the Hedgehog Protector' on the reverse.

The boy looked up and saw this very shiny, round-shaped, gold-metal badge.

It was fantastic.

"Please stand…" she said.

The hedgehog queen gently attached this to Allister's jacket.

Then she continued to speak, "I asked Hamish to go and find us an honest, polite, quiet, animal-loving and above all very caring, special little child, and he found you."

"Good job, Hamish. You really are the MAGIC HEDGEHOG. Good work, my friend." She nodded and smiled.

"Alistair," said the hedgehog queen, "with this little

badge, you will always be able to find me, and it will now be possible for you to protect all the hedgehogs in all the world. Bless you, little Alistair," the hedgehog queen whispered gently.

"I love you all and will always protect you. Wow! Wow!" Alistair said excitedly.

"Thank you so much," said the proud young boy.

Then all the hedgehogs cheered and cheered.

The party continued, and Allister had a great birthday party.

The little boy awoke turned over in his bed and sat up quickly. His mind was racing with thoughts of… last night?

"Was it last night?" he asked himself.

His mother entered the room.

"Happy birthday, Allister," she said.

She was carrying a pile of cards and a pile of presents.

Shortly Allister's father arrived in the room.

The little boy ripped open his cards, not really reading them. Then he ripped and tore his way through the presents.

He had a football, some chocolates, some music albums, socks, a little bag, and a notebook and a pen.

He thanked his mum and dad. They hugged him and informed him that breakfast would be ready soon, and they left him to get dressed.

He was happy but also a little sad as he was trying to think what had happened to him last night. *Was it a dream?*

"Where are those hedgehogs?" he questioned himself over and over.

Then, panic. "My badge, my badge! Where is it? Where is it?"

He looked around the room and under his bed frantically.

"What are you looking for?" asked his mother as she returned to the room.

"Nothing," he replied. "I think I was dreaming last night," he said sadly.

Disappointment was beginning to take over him when, there it was! *WOW, it is real.*

The badge was under the bottom corner of his pillow.

He grabbed it, squeezed it tight and held it against his chest. He smiled widely and gave a little chuckle. So, he was very pleased.

He got dressed quickly ran downstairs and went to the breakfast table.

He was not really hungry, of course, as he had been eating at the party, his party – yes, the hedgehog party.

He looked out of the window. He frowned and said, "That is strange? The air is white.

He really wanted to go out and see the hedgehog house and see what had happened."

"Would the hedgehog house be there? Would it still be so big? Would the hedgehogs be there?"

This all got the better of him and he got up from the table and ran outside.

Yes, the air was white with fog. It was thick.

He could not see more than an arm's length in front of him

He looked down at his feet: he had no shoes on; the ground was very cold. He grabbed some shoes from inside the door.

The grass was hard and made a light crunching sound when walked on. It had turned white.

"This is strange? What is going on?" he questioned.

He made his way to the hedgehog house with speed but…

It was not there. The garden was very quiet and cloudy, with crispy grass and white bushes, and it was cold, very cold. He shuddered.

He began to search frantically for Hamish, or any hedgehog.

Nothing. No hedgehog house… no peanuts… no hedgehogs… no sparkle.

Not a sign that they had ever been there.

The little boy's head dropped with a little sadness.

The little boy became very cold and needed to return to his house.

He turned and walked back slowly, a little sad, but then he put his hand in his trouser pocket, grabbed his badge and looked at it. This made him smile.

"It was all true, then," he said and he was very happy again.

He returned to his home through the thick fog and the first frost that had visited he's garden.

It was now autumn.

The little boy closed the back door behind him.

At that very moment, a very small hedgehog entered the misty garden from under the gate.

The little boy picked up his notebook and pen that he had received for his birthday and began to write.

'A hedgehog story...'